To my sibs, Leonard, Darrell, and Rhonda, with love. —SL

Published by
MAGINATION PRESS
An Educational Publishing Foundation Book
American Psychological Association
750 First Street, NE
Washington, DC 20002

For more information about our books, including a complete catalog,
please write to us, call 1-800-374-2721, or visit our website at
www.apa.org/pubs/magination.

Book design: Susan K. White
Printed by Worzalla, Stevens Point, WI

Library of Congress Cataloging-in-Publication Data

Levins, Sandra.
Bumblebee bike / by Sandra Levins ; illustrated by Claire Keay.
pages cm
"American Psychological Association."
"An Educational Publishing Foundation Book."
Summary: David has a box full of things he borrowed from people without
asking, but when his bicycle is stolen he realizes how wrong he was and
decides it is time to give everything back. Includes note to parents.
ISBN 978-1-4338-1645-1 (hardcover) — ISBN 1-4338-1645-8 (hardcover) —
ISBN 978-1-4338-1646-8 (pbk.) — ISBN 1-4338-1646-6 (pbk.)
(1. Stealing—Fiction. 2. Bicycles—Fiction. 3. Behavior—Fiction.)
I. Keay, Claire, illustrator. II. Title.
PZ7.L5792Bum 2013
(E)—dc23   2013020805

Manufactured in the United States of America
First printing October 2013
10 9 8 7 6 5 4 3 2 1

Bumblebee Bike

by Sandra Levins

illustrated by Claire Keay

MAGINATION PRESS · WASHINGTON, DC

American Psychological Association

David was impatient.
When he saw something he wanted,
his teeth clenched. His fists tightened.
His heart raced. When he wanted
something, he wanted it right away.

David tip-toed to his bedroom,
looking both ways to check that
Mom was nowhere in sight.
He closed his bedroom door and
listened for the click of the latch.

Squeeeak

David opened the closet and dropped to his knees.

"'Scuze me, Elton Don," he whispered.

Elton Don was more than a floppy-eared friend. He was camouflage.
The shoebox he rested on was David's treasure chest.

His heart thumping, David unzipped his backpack
and reached inside.

He felt it. Smooth and slick. Superman. The sparkly
red cape shimmered. One word escaped his lips.

"Cool."

David felt a little guilty. Superman belonged to his best friend Payton. David borrowed it. Well, he sort of borrowed it. He borrowed it without asking. When David saw Payton's Superman, he felt his teeth clench. His fists tighten. His heart race. He wanted it right away.

David and Payton played together all morning, but David's mind was on that sparkly cape. Those red boots. That big red **S**.

When Payton's mom called, "Lunch is ready," David hung back. This was his chance. He snatched Superman faster than a speeding bullet.

David added Superman to the collection of things he had borrowed without asking.

He pressed a button to start the blinking red nose on Aunt Rhonda's reindeer pin.

He whirled a St. Patrick's Day pencil between his palms. It belonged to his teacher, Mr. Jude. The green feathery top puffed like a dandelion.

An apple-size jack-o'-lantern grinned just like it had on Mrs. James's porch.

He squeezed a tiny rubber ball and remembered the day he and his neighbor Charlie bounced it higher than her house.
David planned to cut it open to see what was inside.

He told himself that he would give it all back someday.
Well, maybe not the ball if it was cut in half.

Yet, there was no treasure in the world that he cared about more than his bicycle. It was a dazzling yellow with knobby tires and a bumblebee-striped seat. His bumblebee bike.

Every morning David
pedaled in circles around
his driveway making giant
figure eights.

Every afternoon David, Mom, and baby
Macie rode together to the park.

Every evening
David and Dad
explored trails near
their home.

Dad always reminded David to put his bike in the garage.
"You don't want your bumblebee to disappear."

One awful morning David discovered that his bike was missing!
Horrified, he remembered that he had left it outside.
Someone had taken his bumblebee bike.

David felt sick. Why would someone take something
that belonged to someone else?

His stomach churned. He remembered his secret stash.
The treasures he borrowed without asking.

As Dad filed a police report, David sulked in his room.
It felt absolutely rotten to have something taken this way.

But David felt double absolutely rotten, because he knew that
others felt absolutely rotten because of things he had done.

He kicked a soccer ball in circles around the driveway and made a giant figure eight, but it wasn't the same.

He and Mom pushed Macie in her stroller, but it wasn't the same.

He tossed a football with Dad, but it wasn't the same.

And because he felt double absolutely rotten, he avoided Payton and Charlie. When they knocked on his door, he peeked out and said, **"Go away."**

He avoided Mrs. James, too, pretending not to hear when she called his name.

At school he acted busy and didn't look Mr. Jude in the eye.

One evening, Aunt Rhonda stopped by.
David took a deep breath. He wanted to make this right.

"Aunt Rhonda," he stammered, "I have something that belongs to you. I borrowed it without asking. I'm sorry."

Aunt Rhonda hugged him close. He didn't wriggle away as usual.

David set out to return each treasure to its rightful owner.

Each time, he said, "I have something that belongs to you.
I borrowed it without asking. I'm sorry."

Mrs. James said,
"Well, I'll be!
I thought
the wind blew
that little
pumpkin away."

Payton said, "I wondered what happened to that guy.
If you'd asked, I would have let you borrow him."

"I thought I lost it," said Charlie, who was glad to get her ball back before he cut it in half.

Mr. Jude ruffled David's hair.

David still felt crummy about his bike, but as his backpack lightened up, so did his heart.

A few days later a police car pulled into their driveway.
David gulped. Was he going to be arrested?

The officer popped the trunk and,
with a broad smile, lifted out David's bike.

"This look familiar?"

It was muddy, had weeds in the spokes,
and an ugly scuff on the striped seat.
Yet, it was definitely his bumblebee!

As he and Dad hosed off mud and pulled out weeds, Mom handed David a small gift bag. Inside was a miniature license plate with his name on it: **DAVID**

Mom said, "Now everyone will know who the bumblebee belongs to."

"Yep," said David, "and I know what belongs to me."

Note to Parents and Caregivers

by Mary Lamia, PhD

Has your child ever "borrowed" something without asking permission? In other words, taken or stolen something that wasn't his? While such actions are a normal part of childhood development, it is extremely frustrating for parents and caregivers who have children with sticky fingers! Children may understand *intellectually* that they shouldn't borrow without asking, but they are *emotionally* motivated so they do it anyway.

However, with careful guidance and modeling, children can learn to consciously evaluate and regulate their emotional responses and decide if it would be a good idea to act on them. Kids can think before acting and learn boundaries to develop positive and ethical relationships with others.

How This Book Can Help

In *Bumblebee Bike,* when David saw his friend Payton's Superman, he wanted it. He wanted it right away! David knew that taking what belonged to others was wrong, but he did it anyway. In fact, David had borrowed so much from others that he had a hidden treasure box filled with ill-gotten booty. As adults, we think that this knowledge, and the expectation of consequences, should have stopped him from taking the toy. However, an intellectual understanding of right and wrong is a fragile barrier for a child who is emotionally driven to acquire something he wants. When motivated by their emotions, children have to learn to consider their actions carefully, including asking to borrow or play with a new toy rather than taking it without asking.

When behavior—such as taking something without asking—breaches a boundary, children may experience guilt and shame. It's possible that David's hiding the stolen items in his treasure box was part of a shame response, since shame creates secrecy. A child who is experiencing guilt or shame may try to escape the feeling rather than learn from it. At such times, you as the parent or caregiver can help by teaching responsibility, connecting with your child, and helping him tolerate and learn from the experience. These early experiences of guilt and shame can be an opportunity to help children develop empathy and a capacity to care about the consequences of their actions.

How to Help Your Child Develop Ethical Behavior

In the story, David is motivated to stop borrowing without asking when someone takes his bumblebee bike. But what can you do to help your child change his behavior? Although many young children can recognize that taking something that belongs to someone else is "wrong," they may not yet have developed a capacity for actual moral reflection. While frustrating to you as a parent or caregiver, this behavior is a normal part of childhood development that will likely resolve itself as your child grows older. In the meantime, there are some steps you can take to help your child develop an interest in appropriate social behavior and understand that doing so feels best.

Distinguish between thinking and feeling. As you read the story with your child, ask him to consider what David thinks about his "borrowing without asking" as well as how he *feels*. Note that the emotions motivating David were not wrong, but that his actions made others feel bad and eventually made him feel bad about himself. You may ask your child, "How do you think borrowing without asking made David feel? What could he have done that would make him feel better?"

Brainstorm other options. Ask your child what David might have done differently, given his interest and excitement about the things that did not belong to him. You can say, "When you are interested in something that does not belong to you, what can you do? How would that make others feel? How would it make you feel about yourself?"

Talk about emotions. Help your child to recognize if he is ashamed. Does he withdraw, avoid, or does he lash out on others or himself? Remind your child that acknowledging what he feels and understanding and accepting why he feels that way will help soothe the uncomfortable feelings associated with shame (and help him feel less ashamed). If your child feels ashamed because of his own wrongdoing, separate what he has done from who he is as a person. For example, you may say something like, "I know you feel bad for taking Tommy's toy. It was not a good thing to do. But you're not a bad person just because you did something wrong."

Plan how to make amends. Discuss how the main character in *Bumblebee Bike* was able to recognize his own wrongdoing in discovering how he felt when something of his own was stolen. Ask your child what he can do when his behavior has hurt another person. You can suggest a course of action, such as, "Let's return the toy you took and tell Tommy you're sorry. You'll start feeling better if you try to make this right."

Be a role model. Being a role model will help your child expect respect and trustworthiness in himself and in his relationships with others. Talk to your child about how you respect other people's belongings and expect other people to respect yours. You may even point out situations in books, movies, or television shows when a character takes something that doesn't belong to him. Ask your child how this behavior might make the character feel about himself, and how it might affect his relationships with others.

Behavior that tests the boundaries of social relationships is a normal part of a child's development. In all likelihood, you are the best resource for teaching your child socially appropriate, ethical behavior. However, if your child's behavior continues, or if you would like additional advice, it may be helpful to consult a licensed psychologist or psychotherapist.

Mary Lamia, PhD, is a clinical psychologist and psychoanalyst in Marin County, California. She is also a professor at the Wright Institute in Berkeley, California. She is the author of Understanding Myself: A Kid's Guide to Intense Emotions and Strong Feelings *and* Emotions! Making Sense of Your Feelings, *both published by Magination Press.*

About the Author

Sandra Levins lives in Burlington, Iowa with her husband, Jim.
Their diverse family includes five sons, their partners,
and five adorable grandchildren.

She is the author of award-winning books such as *Eli's Lie-O-Meter:
A Story About Telling the Truth; Was It the Chocolate Pudding?
A Story For Little Kids About Divorce;* and *Do You Sing Twinkle?
A Story About Remarriage and New Family,*
also published by Magination Press.

About the Illustrator

Claire Keay lives in the south of England where she works from
her small studio at home illustrating children's books and greeting
cards as well as designing her own range of digital craft products.

About Magination Press

Magination Press is an imprint of the American Psychological
Association, the largest scientific and professional organization
representing psychologists in the United States and the largest
association of psychologists worldwide.